Thomas Jefferson
and the Ghostriders

ALADDIN PAPERBACKS
An imprint of Simon & Schuster Children's Publishing Division
1230 Avenue of the Americas, New York, NY 10020
Text copyright © 2008 by Howard Goldsmith
Illustrations copyright © 2008 by Drew Rose
All rights reserved, including the right of reproduction
in whole or in part in any form.
READY-TO-READ, CHILDHOOD OF FAMOUS AMERICANS,
ALADDIN PAPERBACKS, and related logo
are registered trademarks of Simon & Schuster, Inc.
Also available in an Aladdin library edition.
Designed by Christopher Grassi
The text of this book was set in Century Old Style.
Manufactured in the United States of America
First Aladdin Paperbacks edition January 2008
6 8 10 9 7 5
Cataloging-in-Publication Data is on file with the Library of Congress.
ISBN-13: 978-1-4169-2692-4 (pbk.)
ISBN-10: 1-4169-2692-5 (pbk.)
ISBN-13: 978-1-4169-2749-5 (lib. bdg.)
ISBN-10: 1-4169-2749-2 (lib. bdg.)
0115 LAK

Thomas Jefferson
and the Ghostriders

By Howard Goldsmith
Illustrated by Drew Rose

Ready-to-Read
ALADDIN
New York London Toronto Sydney

Tom Jefferson grew up in Virginia.
He was a tall boy with red hair and
freckles.

One day Tom found his father's map of Virginia. A Native American burial mound was marked in red.

Tom saw it was located in the woods beyond his home. Curious, Tom asked his father about the burial mound.

"Do not ever go near that spot!"

his father warned.

"It is a holy place."

A boy told Tom the woods were haunted.
"I saw ghosts ride by on tall horses,"
he said. "Do not let them catch you!"
Tom's friend, Dabney Carr, laughed at
the boy. "I do not believe in ghosts,"
Dabney said.

"Let us go out tonight, Tom! I am not scared. I dare you to go with me!" said Dabney.

"I am not scared either," Tom said.

That night the two boys sneaked into the forest. A bright full moon hung in the sky.

A hawk stared at them with
flaming red eyes.
Ke-wee-wee!
it warned.

The boys ran along the Rivanna River.
After an hour they came to the area on
the map.

Suddenly the burial mound

rose up before them.

It was a twelve-foot-high hill.

"Gosh!" Tom said, swallowing hard.

In the next moment they heard
twigs snapping and horses galloping.
Dabney grabbed Tom's shirtsleeve
and held on tightly.

"The ghosts are coming!" he cried.

"They don't sound like ghosts,"

Tom said. "They sound like riders."

The boys leaped behind a bush and watched. A long line of riders moved toward the burial mound.

The chief sat on top of a tall, white horse.

The men stopped and prayed silently.

Tom and Dabney did not dare to speak.
Then Dabney whispered, "Let us go,
Tom. It is getting cold."

"All right," Tom answered. "Thank goodness the men did not see us."

As Tom rose to leave, the chief turned his head and winked at Tom with a smile.

Dabney ran off like a rabbit.

Instead of running,

Tom smiled back at the chief.

"He will not hurt us!"

Tom called after Dabney.

Tom understood these men did not
harm children. As Tom hurried after
Dabney, the chief called out.

Tom stopped and turned.

Tom did not understand the chief's
language. But he knew the chief
meant "Go in peace."

The next day Tom visited the Native American village. The people were friendly to Tom.

They showed him how to plant seeds
and grow corn.

From that day on, Tom learned
to like and respect people
of all kinds.
They all had much to offer.
When he grew up, Tom always
remembered those friendly people.

He thought, *Everyone has something good to give and to get from this county. We can all live side by side in peace. We can learn from one another and share the wonderful gifts of America.*

In 1776 Thomas Jefferson became famous for writing the Declaration of Independence. In 1801 he became the third president of the United States.

Here is a time line of Thomas Jefferson's life:

1743	Born on April 13 in Virginia
1769	Elected to the Virginia House of Burgesses
1772	Married Martha Wayles Skelton
1776	Wrote the Declaration of Independence, dated July 4, 1776
1779	Elected governor of Virginia
1782	Wife, Martha, died on September 6
1785–1789	Minister to France
1790–1793	Secretary of state under President George Washington
1797–1801	Vice president of the United States
1801–1809	President of the United States
1803	Doubled the size of the United States with the Louisiana Purchase
1804	Sent the Lewis and Clark expedition to the West
1809	Returned to his home, Monticello
1826	Died on July 4 at Monticello at age eighty-three